THE
WAR
AND
FREDDY

THE
WAR
AND
FREDDY

DENNIS HAMLEY

Illustrated by George Buchanan

CATNIP BOOKS
Published by Catnip Publishing Ltd.
14 Greville Street
London
EC1N 8SB

This edition published 2007
1 3 5 7 9 10 8 6 4 2

A CIP catalogue record for this book is available from the British Library

ISBN 978-1-84647-041-7

Printed in Poland

www.catnippublishing.co.uk

Another one for the Offley Gang

Contents

1939 – 1940
Freddy and the Start of It   1

Spring 1941
Freddy and Three Sorts of Water   10

Summer to Autumn, 1941
Freddy and the Reading Problem   22

Spring 1942
Freddy and the Unexploded Bomb   35

Autumn 1942
Freddy and the Spy   45

Spring 1943
Freddy and the War Games   56

Christmas 1943
Freddy and the Meccano Set   71

Spring to Summer, 1944
Freddy and the Prisoners of War   84

1945
Freddy and the End of It   101

Freddy and the Start of It

Millions of people lived through the start of the war and never forgot it.

Freddy lived through it and never knew a thing. But then, he was only three.

One day nearly a year afterwards – though he didn't know that either – he looked out of the window at the railway station. He got a big surprise.

Every day he watched the trains. They were all green. Always.

But today, there were new colours. Some were dark red. Some had green engines and cream and brown carriages. Some had carriages which looked as though they were made of shiny wood.

And there were so many of them. They were all going the same way. Towards the sea.

"Mummy, look at the trains," he said.

"They're going to fetch the soldiers," Mummy answered.

Next day the trains came back. Slowly they crept through the station; all day, all night. A few stopped. Freddy saw dark green lorries with red crosses painted on white circles lined up outside the station.

When Mummy took him for a walk down to the town, he saw lots of strange men. They stood in little groups. They wore rough, greeny-brown clothes.

Some of the words they said he could understand. But
their voices were strange. Some were gruff. Some were
sharp. Some were sing-song. They looked at him with
hollow, sad eyes. They seemed worn-out.

Freddy was frightened.

"Who are they, Mummy?" he said.

"The soldiers home from the war," she answered.

"What's the war?"

He waited a long time for the answer as they walked
to the shops.

"Some people who live a long way away are cross with us," Mummy said at last. "We're cross with them as well. So we're having a war."

Wars, thought Freddy, must be everywhere. Mr Binstead next door was always cross with Daddy. Daddy was cross with him back. Who knew why? Crossness was part of the world. But why should it lead to sad, tired men coming to their town in long, slow trains?

A few months later, the war did something else. It brought Freddy's bed downstairs. It brought Mummy and Daddy downstairs as well. They slept on little camp beds in the living room with him.

The war also brought strange wailing noises outside at night.

"Sirens," said Daddy. "Air raid warnings."

It brought humming, growling noises overhead.

"The bombers are going to London," said Mummy.

The bombers went to London night after night and Freddy felt a strange excitement when he heard them.

One night, as the growly hum went on overhead, the house shook suddenly and there was a great roaring noise. Soot fell out of the chimney all over Freddy's bed.

Next morning, when the mess was cleared up, Mummy and Daddy took Freddy across dewy fields as the sun rose. Everybody who lived in the road was with them. They all stood round a wide, deep, smoking

pit next to Farmer Crellin's fields which wasn't there the night before. Daddy and Mr Binstead stood side by side and weren't cross with each other at all.

"Fancy taking all that trouble just to make a hole in the ground," said someone.

Now Freddy found things out.

The people we were cross with were called the Jerries. They flew over the sea to us in strange aeroplanes. These aeroplanes were ugly, with square wings and spiky black crosses painted on them. One was called "the flying pencil".

We had lovely aeroplanes with round wings with coloured circles on them. Ours were best but they had more.

The Jerries had another name. It sounded like "Nasties" and Freddy thought this must be right because they obviously were.

One day he saw very close a square-winged aeroplane with crosses on. He was playing in the garden. There was a sudden terrible noise and the black plane flew low and very fast over him. Then a round-winged plane with circles followed it. Low and very fast.

He wasn't a bit frightened. He wanted to join in the chase. He knew their names now. He jumped up and down, waving his arms and shouting.

"Messerschmitt and Spitfire. Messerschmitt and Spitfire."

Joy flooded through him as the two aeroplanes climbed high into the sky, the Spitfire still chasing.

But not for long. The back door was flung open. Mummy dashed out in her apron. She seized him

round the shoulders and smacked his legs hard. Then she dragged him indoors. He was too shocked to cry. She flung him on to a chair. Then she leaned with her face against the wall and cried and cried. Her shoulders shook. When he tried to go up close to her, she pushed him away.

Freddy didn't need to know why.

"It's the war," he said sadly, and crept upstairs.

Freddy loved the gas masks. They made the grown-ups look funny, like little elephants with their trunks chopped off.

The one he had been given was white with a Mickey Mouse face on it. Wearing it made him hot. His voice sounded tinny and the eyepiece misted up so he couldn't see. But when he put it on with the little tin hat Daddy had given him for his fourth birthday and when he slung his rifle, made from a broomstick with a wooden handle and an old belt for a sling, over his shoulder, he knew he was in the war and the war was his.

So he walked out of the front door and joined the South Road Army. All the children in the road were in it. The leader was one of the big boys. He was nearly ten. He wore a real army forage cap and carried an airgun.

His name was Michael. He formed the children up in three straight lines and shouted "Ten-*shun*" and "Stand *easy*" and "Quick *march*" at them till one by

one they realized what he wanted them to do. Then they shuffled up and down the road, arms swinging wildly. A passer-by said, "Look at them. I bet they'd scare Hitler half to death," and they all smartened up and felt very good.

By this time, though, the Mickey Mouse gas mask had misted up so much that Freddy couldn't see where he was going. He tripped over the edge of the pavement and cut his knee open. So he had to be temporarily invalided out of the South Road Army.

Just after that, a big envelope plopped through the letter-box. Daddy opened it.

"It's here. Call-up," he said.

His parents looked at each other. Freddy looked at them. He saw their eyes were wide.

"Daddy's got to go in the army," said Mummy.

Freddy looked hard at his father's familiar round face and his sandy hair with the centre parting. He listened to his voice as he said, "That's right, son. You'll be the man of the house now." He thought – Is *he* going to have sad eyes and talk in a funny way like the soldiers in town on the day of the trains?

Daddy went away on the train in his ordinary clothes and carrying a little case.

To Freddy, it seemed years before he came back for a few days. He looked older, thinner, taller. His khaki uniform was smarter than those of the soldiers in the town. He had a kitbag and big boots which were very shiny. But his voice hadn't changed a bit.

Freddy didn't know what to feel. Should he be sad because his father was now part of a dangerous world far away? Or should he be proud because the fathers of other members of the South Road Army were away at the war and now he was as good as any of them?

Daddy didn't keep his uniform on for long. For the few days he was with them he wore his ordinary clothes and Freddy was disappointed.

Then one day, Daddy polished the boots and buttons so they gleamed even more, packed his kitbag, put his uniform on and spoke to Freddy.

He said, "You won't see me for a good while now, Freddy. You'll be a big boy when I come back, so look after your mother for me while I'm gone. I'm relying on you."

And then he was away on the train.

And then Freddy knew all about the war. Nothing would be the same again.

Freddy and
Three Sorts of Water

Sometimes, Freddy remembered things which happened before the war started. There were lights in the streets at night, no criss-cross sticky tape over windows and Daddy was at home.

There was another memory which kept coming to him. It was blue and gold and the sun was on his back. The blue stretched as far as he could see and

it shooshed towards him over the gold. There were photos to prove he was there. The photos were grey, but he could still see the blue and gold.

"The sea," said Mummy. "We went there for holidays. We can't go now. There's a war on."

But after Daddy had gone away for the second time, Mummy took Freddy to Granny and Grandad Crake's. They were Mummy's parents and lived deep in the country. Freddy and Mummy sat for hours in a wheezy green train and then bumped along in an old bus with wooden seats. Then they were there.

Freddy was pleased. He liked Granny and Grandad Crake. Granny Crake was small and white-haired. She looked frail. Grandad Crake was small as well, but wiry and strong. His sharp little face was burnt brown from being outdoors and nearly all his hair was gone.

Their house was funny. It had no upstairs. There were trees all round it. It was also near the sea.

"Can we go to the sea?" asked Freddy.

"I can't afford it," said Mummy.

Sea or no sea, the little house in the country was exciting. There was a big black kitchen range. There was a fireplace with shiny tongs and pokers in the hearth. There was a wooden shed with a workbench, tools and paints in it. Though water came through the taps, there was a big steel tank outside which caught rain water from the gutters.

And there was a well.

Freddy was sad at what Mummy had said. No sea. The tank and the well would have to do. On the first evening he went outside to look at them.

The well was best. It was a great dark hole in the ground. A low brick wall was built in a ring all round it. There was a little tiled roof and a big handle. The handle had a spindle coiled with fraying grey rope. Freddy couldn't move the handle however hard he tried.

Far below in the blackness at the end of the rope was a bucket.

Freddy leaned over the wall. He sniffed. A damp, musty smell came up to greet his nose. He strained his

eyes to see the well's bottom. He could see the brick lining for a few feet – then pitch black.

Freddy leaned further over.

Suddenly, he was pulled backwards. The shock gave him a fright.

Mummy was there, very cross.

"You come away from there," she said. "It's not safe."

She dragged him in. Freddy felt very annoyed. He wasn't doing anything wrong. But he knew his mother. There was no point in arguing.

Besides, it was Grandad Crake Mummy was really cross with.

"You want to fill that old well in, Dad," she said. "Freddy could fall over the edge."

"I need it," said Grandad Crake. "What if Jerry drops a bomb on the waterworks? I'd have the only water for miles around."

That night, Freddy dreamed about the wide, blue waters of the sea and the dark, still waters trapped in the well.

When he woke up he had a thought. The well was just a black hole. So how did Grandad Crake *know* there was water down there?

After breakfast, when Mummy wasn't looking, Freddy went to the well again.

First, he tried the handle. He managed to get it to make a squeaky noise but it still wouldn't move. The grey rope, he saw, was furry and fraying.

He looked over the edge again.

Then he picked up a little pebble. He dropped it over the side and counted: "One, two, three." Then: "plop."

Yes, there was water there.

He found a bigger stone, leaned over and dropped it. One – two – three. A real splash this time, and an extra little swooshing noise. The stone had made a wave which hit the well sides.

This was good. Freddy went off to look again and came back with a brick. Over it went; one – two – three. The big splash this time echoed round the well and up the hole. The noise of waves against the sides lasted a long time before all was still again.

Bigger stones were needed. Freddy went in search.

At the end of the garden, Grandad Crake had made a rockery. Freddy spied a big white rock which looked ideal. He just managed to lift it. He staggered four paces and then fell down.

This was no good. Freddy went in search again. In the shed, he found Grandad Crake's wheelbarrow. Soon, the stone was in the barrow and the barrow was by the well. Freddy heaved the stone out and lifted it to the top of the wall. It balanced there; then Freddy touched it gently with the tips of his fingers. To his surprise and absolute delight it toppled over the side. Freddy counted: "One, two –" No splash. But a great crash of metal and a big scraping noise that echoed round the well. The handle turned for a second, then stopped. The rope jerked and, just below the handle, parted. A frayed end hung loose, the rest disappeared. "Three," Freddy gasped.

Now there was a splash that was truly terrific. It was like a depth charge. Freddy had seen them at the

pictures, in films about the navy. Spray came right up the well, hit him in the face and wetted the ground all around.

He leaned fascinated over the wall and heard the waves churning away far below, slowly dying away.

Mummy and Grandad Crake heard as well. They came running.

"He's lost my bucket," shrieked Grandad Crake. "He's sent it to the bottom. We'll have no water when Jerry comes. Drat the boy."

Mummy didn't speak. She just dragged Freddy indoors and that – for him – was the end of the day.

That night, he dreamed about the bucket lying

in the dark, still water, the broken rope still tied to its handle. It was there for ever. He was with it. The dream frightened him.

Next morning, he found Grandad Crake had made a fence of rope and sticks round the well. So he went instead to the water tank.

This too had a satisfying smell. He trailed his fingers to and fro and watched the wake they cut through the water. He dropped little stones in and saw how fast they fell through the air and how slowly they fell through the water.

Two minutes later, he was fed up with stones.

So he found two small pieces of wood in Grandad Crake's shed and floated them in the tank. One, he decided, was to be *Ark Royal*, the other the *Bismarck*. The *Ark Royal* kept ramming the *Bismarck*, so hard that splinters were knocked off both of them. Then Freddy got the *Bismarck* trapped against the side of the tank while *Ark Royal* ran full tilt into it again and again, harder and harder. But still the *Bismarck* floated there. *Ark Royal* turned it upside down, pushed it under nose first till it stood straight up in the air, knocked it over on its side. Still it came back and still it floated.

In the end, Freddy had to sink the *Bismarck* by holding it under water. But when his arm got cold and he had to let go, the *Bismarck* came straight to the surface and floated there once more, laughing at him.

Freddy let it.

He trailed his fingers again in the water, watching them beneath the surface.

Then his eyes widened. Something was wrong with his fingers.

He pushed his arm in. Something was wrong with his arm.

Where it entered the water, it was bent. As if someone had tried to pull it out of its joint. But he felt no pain. Only cold. What was the water doing?

He moved his arm gently up and down in the water. Yes. Amazing. First his elbow was bent, then his forearm, then his wrist, then his fingers again. And he never felt a thing.

Bent fingers, unsinkable ships – water was amazing stuff.

And he was fed up with it.

Because really he was so *bored*. Wells and water tanks, the house in the country and Grandad's shed couldn't make up for all his friends back at home. He was excited at coming. But now he was here – and especially if they weren't going to the seaside – *there was nothing to do*.

That night, he dreamed about the *Bismarck* really sinking to the bottom of the sea, where it joined the bucket. Then he dreamed about the sea itself, blue lapping the gold and only a bus ride away that Mummy couldn't afford to make.

His dream turned into something very real in which Mummy stood over his bed, saying, "Wake up, Freddy. We're going to the seaside." But all the time he knew he was asleep.

The door opened, someone drew the curtains and light flooded in.

"Wake up, Freddy," said Mummy.

Freddy opened his eyes.

"We're going to the seaside," said Mummy.

They went on the bus. When they got off, Freddy looked up the street. At the end was a gap. In the gap was nothing but what looked like a line drawn across the sky. Above the line was light grey; below, a darker grey.

"You can see the sea already, Freddy," said Mummy.

"Why isn't it blue?" said Freddy.

"The sun's in," said Grandad Crake. "It's too cloudy. Don't you kids know anything any more?"

They walked at Granny Crake's slow place up the road to the sea front. The day was cold. There were few people around. The shooshing noise of the waves grew louder.

And then they were there. A shingle beach curved round in front of them. The calm sea lapped at the stones, sucked them back and threw them forward.

Freddy started to run towards the wonderful sight. Then he stopped.

Between Freddy and the sea were rolls and rolls of barbed wire. On either side they stretched, as far as the eye could see. Nobody could go on the beach.

"The barbed wire's in case the Jerries come," said Grandad Crake.

"I can't go in the sea," cried Freddy in despair.

"Of course you can't," said Grandad Crake. "There's a war on."

"Why didn't you tell us before we came, Dad?" said Mummy. She sounded very cross.

"Why should I? You have to see these things for yourself," said Grandad Crake.

Freddy stared. He nearly cried.

Then, even clearer than before they came to Granny and Grandad Crake's house, he remembered things before the war. Things that happened when he was very small. Things in the photographs.

He remembered sand between his toes, waves round his feet. He remembered sitting in the breakers while the water rushed very fast past him one way and then came back again, full of bubbles which burst as they passed him. And he remembered the sun on his back.

And he thought, One day, Daddy will be home and the war will be gone and they'll take the barbed wire away and I'll sit in the sea again.

But for now – he sighed – I'll have to make do with the well and the water tank.

Summer to Autumn, 1941

Freddy and
the Reading Problem

Freddy often looked out of the window at the trains going by. There were little ones with green tank engines and only two carriages. There were big ones with huge green engines and lots of carriages. Freddy didn't know how many. Soon he would go to school to find out how to count to more than three.

Often they stopped right opposite the window, at a signal, just where he could see them. Smoke would come out of their funnels. They would make an angry roaring noise as if cross at being held up. Then they would give a loud, shrieky whistle.

"OOOORRRRP!"

Freddy would lean out of the window and answer them.

"OOOORRRRP!"

One of them had taken Daddy away. Another would one day bring him back. Often Freddy wondered which one it would be.

Summer was nearly over. It was time for Freddy to make a journey of his own. He was going to school.

One morning, Mummy dressed him in his blue overcoat and slung the Mickey Mouse gas mask over his shoulder.

"You'll be staying at school till you're nearly grown up," said Mummy. "I'll come to take you home at the end of the afternoon."

That didn't make sense to Freddy. Surely school wasn't such a magic place that he would be a big boy by four o'clock. That didn't bear thinking about. He decided he would be a train.

"OOOORRRRP!" he said.

School was a funny place. Mummy walked him down the road and through the big gates. There he stood in a grey playground. Thousands of girls and boys, all huge, ran dangerously round him. They shouted so loud he was deafened.

Suddenly he hoped he *would* be grown up by four o'clock.

Then he was pulled into the school. Inside, it was quiet. There were high windows, little desks in rows to sit at and a funny smell. Mummy brought him to a tall lady with brown hair who also had a funny, though nicer, smell.

"Hello, Freddy," she said. "I'm Miss Binks. Here are the other children new today."

They were all sitting on the floor. Freddy sat with them. Stella and Tony were there from the South Road Army. He had never seen any of the others before.

Mummy bent down and kissed him on the forehead.

"Goodbye, Freddy," she said. "Be a good boy."
Then she left. Freddy looked round the room.
"OOOORRRRP!" he said.

The worst thing about the day was that Miss Binks
didn't like him saying "OOOORRRRP!" Or anything
else.

But he was pleased he was still the same size when
Mummy met him at the school gate. As they walked
home, he thought of Daddy. A big green train clanked
by and Freddy could see people looking out of the
windows.

"Daddy might be on that," he said hopefully.
"Oh, no," said Mummy. "You know where he is.
He's thousands of miles away. In a hot place called
North Africa. In the desert."

Freddy had his tea, listened to the wireless and went to bed early. He dreamed of funny smells, green trains and hot places.

Mummy listened to the news on the wireless a lot. So did Freddy. He didn't understand it much. But now he began to listen for the places Mummy had told him about. North Africa. The desert. Once he started listening, he heard about them a lot.

Mummy was also always looking at the newspaper. So did Freddy. He looked at the pictures. But they weren't as good as the ones in his picture books. He looked at drawings of strange shapes with black arrows on them which Mummy called "maps". He couldn't see what they were supposed to be. And then he looked at the lines and lines and lines of squiggles all over the pages. One day he would know all about them. That was why he was going to school. But now, they made his heart sink.

He had a book at school. He tried to read it. He couldn't.

Miss Binks wrote letters on the blackboard. Everybody said them. Freddy said what the others said a split second afterwards. He couldn't see how a squiggle could be a noise as well. It was a long way from here to the newspaper. And even further to North Africa.

Stella could read a book. She read it aloud to Miss Binks. Freddy heard her.

Ann has a fan.
Show the fan to Mother, Ann.
Ann ran to show the fan to Mother.
Pat had not a cap.
Ann, run to Mother for a cap for Pat.
Mother had not a cap for Pat.
Mother had a hat.
Thank you Mother for the hat for Pat.

He looked at the page she was reading. How did Stella know that was what it said?

Anyway, what was the point? He didn't care about Ann's fan or Pat's cap or whether he had to make do with a hat.

It was his turn to read to Miss Binks. He stared at the page. It still didn't make sense. He tried to remember what Stella had read. That didn't make sense either.

Miss Binks was cross.

"Come on, Freddy. You aren't trying."

"I am, miss."

He tried to remember the letters Miss Binks wrote on the board. Slowly he started.

"Ann … had … a …"

"Well done, Freddy."

Ten minutes later Freddy had stumbled through the whole page, with Miss Binks telling him nearly everything.

"Good boy." It didn't sound as if she meant it. "Sit down now. Come here, Tony."

He looked again at the page he had just read. It had dissolved into squiggle and meant nothing to him.

Next week, Stella read the new page and Freddy heard her.

> *Father has a top for Pat.*
> *Father has a fan for Ann.*
> *Father and Mother, show the top to Pat.*
> *Father and Mother, show the fan to Ann.*
> *Come for the top, Pat.*
> *Come for the fan, Ann.*
> *Pat and Ann ran for the top and the fan.*

The first word, *Father*. He looked at the page in his book. Yes, that was what "Father" looked like. He thought of Daddy in the hot place. He looked at the Father in the picture, in his grey suit, giving the top to Pat. It wasn't fair.

He turned to read to Miss Binks.

"Father," he said, and stopped.

"Go on, Freddy," said Miss Binks.

He couldn't. He was crying.

"Now then, Freddy," said Miss Binks sternly. "Lots of children here have fathers away at the war. I'm sure your daddy wouldn't like to see you cry."

Freddy tried hard to stop. He managed it and struggled, with Miss Binks mouthing every word for him, through the page. But now he couldn't care less about Pat and Ann and their tops and fans.

He wondered if reading was worth the effort.

Next morning, he listened with Mummy to the news. There was a lot about North Africa and the desert. Then the paper plopped through the letter-box.

Mummy seized it. She looked at the big black writing at the top and the little writing underneath. Then she looked at the strange drawings in little boxes on the front page.

"What are they, Mummy?" asked Freddy.

"Maps. Maps of the desert."

Freddy looked at her. They still meant nothing.

A new page. Stella rattled through it.

> *Sam, Sam. See the dog.*
> *Sit on him if you can.*
> *Sam sat on the dog and the dog ran to Ann.*
> *Ann has a tin.*
> *See Ann tip the tin for the dog.*
> *See the dog dip into the tin.*

Freddy hadn't got a dog. And he didn't believe there had ever been one as big as in the picture. And even if there was he was quite certain it wouldn't let Sam ride it like a horse.

This is a silly page, he thought.

Standing by Miss Binks, he stared at it.

Not a word could he make out.

"I'm getting cross with you, Freddy," said Miss Binks. "You're not trying. I hope I won't have to tell your mother that you have a reading problem."

Freddy looked at Sam who, with a daft grin on his face, sat astride the dog, who had an even dafter grin.

No, reading definitely wasn't worth the effort.

That night, Freddy dreamed again of Daddy in the hot, desert place. He saw his face burnt red by the sun, sweaty and tired. He saw yellow sand and heard guns and aeroplanes. He felt the heat so much that it made him choke. Then he woke up.

Mummy was reading the paper. Freddy looked over her shoulder. First he looked at the map. It had black arrows all over it. Some had swastikas on them. Freddy pointed.

"That's the Germans," he said.

Others had little Union Jacks.

"That's Daddy," said Freddy.

He looked at the arrows again. He saw which way they pointed. Then he cried out in joy.

"Daddy's chasing them all away."

Now he looked intently at the big, black writing. Somewhere in it was Daddy. The writing means Daddy, he thought.

The squiggles were still all jumbled up before his eyes. But Daddy. They meant Daddy. He strained to make sense of them.

He pointed at the first letters.

"O," he said. Then – "U.R." A flash of inspiration. "Our."

He stared again. The next word looked familiar. He had seen it over the door he went through to get inside the school.

"Boys," he said.

He wrinkled his forehead over the next word and then left it. The two which came after he knew easily.

"In. On," he said.

He went back to the one before.

"C," he said. "L."

Mummy had heard him and had come over to where he stood.

"The door's open," she said. "Go and *close* it for me, please."

Freddy did as he was told – but when he got there, turned back in surprise. The door was shut.

"It's shut," he said.

"So you don't have to *close* it after all," Mummy said.

Freddy went crossly back to the letters – then looked up laughing. "Close," he said.

"Of course, you can say those letters another way," said Mummy.

Freddy looked at her despairingly. Reading's bad enough, he thought. Don't make it worse. But he was unhappy only for a second. He knew he was on the edge of great things.

The last word was now quite easy to make out. But it didn't seem to mean anything.

"Tob," said Freddy. Then – "Ruk."

Then the whole thing together.

"*Our boys close in on Tob-ruk.* What does it mean, Mummy? Is it about Daddy?"

"Tobruk," she said, making the last word sound different. "Yes, it is about Daddy."

"He's not a boy."

"They're all boys. To us, they are."

Suddenly, Mummy looked at him with shining eyes.

"Freddy, you can *read*!"

"What else does it say about Daddy?"

"Read it for yourself."

Freddy tried. He didn't get very far.

"Never mind, love," said Mummy. "You've started."

She read the rest of the first page of the paper to him. It didn't mean much. Daddy was never mentioned. But he was in there somewhere and Freddy hung on to every word.

Next day, Miss Binks called Freddy out first to read.

"I hope you do better today," she said.

She opened the book and Freddy looked at the page. Suddenly it was clear.

I am Ann's pet hen.
I am red and fat,
I sit on ten eggs in my pen.
Pat has come to see my eggs.
Pat has his dog with him.
Pat will not let his dog into my pen.

"Well done, Freddy," said Miss Binks in surprise.

Freddy turned round and stuck his tongue out at Stella.

"You'll soon finish this book," said Miss Binks. "Then you can go on to the next."

So what, thought Freddy. Why do I want to know about Ann's hen and Sam sitting on that stupid dog and whether Pat has a cap or a hat? It's all *silly*. It doesn't *mean* anything. I want to get home and look at the paper and find out about Daddy.

As he and Mummy walked home by the railway, a big green train went slowly past and stopped at the signal.

Freddy watched it.

"OOOORRRRP!" said the train.

"No, Freddy," said Mummy. "Daddy won't be on it. Not for a long time yet."

"I know," said Freddy. "But I'll find out when he's coming. I'll keep reading the paper."

The signal changed; the train puffed slowly away.

Freddy watched it go.

"OOOORRRRP!" he said.

Spring 1942

Freddy and the Unexploded Bomb

Michael was the oldest in the South Road Army. That's why he was leader.

Now he was at school, Freddy wasn't the youngest any more. There were Tony, Barry and Kathleen below him. Stella was the same age. Janet, Philip and Tom, Mavis and Enid, Johnny, Betty and Reg were older. Being in the middle made Freddy feel good.

Freddy was a bit afraid of Michael. He had dark brown hair plastered straight over his head and a turned-down mouth as if he was always cross.

Mr Binstead watched him one night as he led the South Road Army past his house.

"When that Michael grows up he'll look just like Hitler," he said.

Everyone in the Army heard. They were all shocked, except Michael. His turned-down mouth for once turned up a little as he managed a secret smile.

Mr Binstead was wearing a khaki uniform. He was off to the Home Guard headquarters. Michael couldn't see why the South Road Army couldn't do the same duties as the Home Guard. Neither could Freddy or any of the rest. A sense of deep unfairness settled on the force each time they marched because

the grown-ups seemed to think they were only playing.

They weren't. They were planning.

Michael had an aircraft recognition book. In it were pages of black silhouettes of planes seen from every angle so you could recognize them at once. He held the book up in front of the South Road Army and exhorted them to spot "one of ours" or "one of theirs".

"What if it's one of theirs?" said Freddy.

Michael had the answer.

"You wait till it flies low," he said. "Then you pick

up a handful of sand and you throw it up in the air as hard as you can so it gets in the propellor and the engine. That will gum up the works and the plane will crash."

Freddy was impressed. Bringing down enemy planes was a lot easier than he had thought.

"Where do we get the sand from?" asked Enid.

"You have to keep it with you all the time," said Michael. "In a bucket."

Carrying buckets full of sand everywhere did not last long. Not a single German plane was brought down.

"The Jerries know what they're doing," said Michael. "They won't come low on purpose."

Morale in the South Road Army was low.

"But there's other things we can do," said Michael. "We can look out for spies. And we can warn people about bombs. Spies leave little bombs around which can blow people up. There's posters about them all over the place."

Indeed there were. Freddy had seen lots.

"So if you see something which looks like a bomb," went on Michael, "come and tell me and I'll do something about it."

Michael stood there, towering over them in his grey shirt and short trousers and Freddy thought: yes, he will, because he is our leader.

Enemy planes didn't come over much now – not like last year – so Freddy could afford to go around with his eyes looking down at the ground rather than combing the skies. So could the rest of the South Road Army. Heads down, fifteen children aged from four to ten walked slowly up and down the road, round their gardens, up the alleyway which led out of the road, across the patch of waste ground beyond the houses and across the fields beyond as far as the bomb crater – now a green weedy pit with rubbish at the bottom.

They did this all afternoon and all evening until mothers came out to call them in and cries of "not yet" and "in a minute" echoed round the road.

Mr Binstead in his uniform watched them and said, "You won't find treasure that way."

Michael looked at him like a young officer surveying

an old sweat and said, "We're not looking for treasure. We're helping the war effort."

Mr Binstead laughed, said "Silly kids" and clumped off to Home Guard HQ.

"Keep looking," shouted Michael, running up and down the road in anger. "Don't mind him." Mr Binstead had riled him. "We'll show them."

But they found nothing that evening and some of the Army were getting as fed up as they were at the end of the anti-aircraft campaign.

"All right," said Michael, who felt he had to make a decision. "We look for bombs till tomorrow afternoon. Then, if we've not found any, we'll think of something else."

Freddy was determined he would be the one to find a bomb. Time was running out so he peered at everything with desperate keenness.

There was nothing in the garden. Nothing down the drains, nothing stuck in hedges or fences. Nothing anywhere.

Now he was rooting around in the long grass on the waste ground. It was nearly time to stop. Nothing here at all.

Then he saw it.

A whitish metal object. About the size of a tin of beans. But white, with a hole at the end. Made of something much thicker than tin. He bent to look closer – then jumped back. No, he remembered. You *mustn't* go near these things.

He stepped even further back and looked at it.

Yes, nestling there in the long grass, a perfect hiding

place. Waiting there, looking innocent, ready to blow him, the South Road Army, Mummy, Mr Binstead, everyone, up in the air. Left, no doubt, by a spy.

What to do? First of all, find Michael.

Freddy turned and ran, shouting at the top of his voice.

"A bomb. I've found a bomb. We're all going to be blown up."

Michael came running. So did the rest. They stood round in a big circle and Michael frowned as he surveyed the object.

"Definitely," he said at last. "That's a bomb if ever I saw one."

He turned to Freddy.

"Well done," he said.

Freddy's heart swelled.

"Who shall we tell?" he said. Michael would know.

But Michael didn't seem to know after all. He scratched his head and thought.

"What about Mr Binstead?" said Freddy. "He's got a uniform."

Mr Binstead was weeding his front garden. He seemed surprised at being besieged by fifteen children and came unwillingly. But when he saw the object …

"Yes," he said. "A bomb. That's a bomb if ever I saw one."

Amazing, thought Freddy. Not only did Michael and Mr Binstead agree, but they even used exactly the same words. It really must be true.

"We need the police and the air raid warden," said Mr Binstead. "I'll get them."

"I'll come with you," said Michael.

For a moment after they left, Freddy felt cheated. Other people had taken his bomb over and left him out. Then he felt proud. Surely he'd get a medal for this. Perhaps some money. His name in the paper.

Three policemen arrived. So did the air raid warden, in his tin hat with ARP written on it. Word had spread round the houses. Everybody was outside. Even so, the policemen ran round blowing whistles and shouting, "Evacuate all houses. Emergency."

Freddy felt even better. This *proved* he'd done a great thing.

Now a big circle of people lined the borders of the

waste ground. The policemen rushed around holding them back. A mutter of frightened talk filled the air. Freddy heard the words, "Why don't they save time and get the army bomb disposal people?"

The air raid warden stepped into the clearing in the middle of the crowd. When they saw him, there was silence. Now some people crept away. They took cover behind walls and fences. Pale faces appeared for a few seconds at a time from behind them, then disappeared.

The air raid warden walked towards the object. The silence crackled.

Freddy looked round at the scene. *He* had done all this. Everybody was there because of him. He felt power. There was *nothing* he couldn't do.

The air raid warden had reached the middle. He got down on hands and knees, squinting at the object. He reached out gingerly for it. The quiet was unbearable.

He bent closer. He looked again. He actually touched it.

Freddy closed his eyes, waiting for the blast.

Nothing happened. Freddy opened his eyes.

The air raid warden was standing up. His face glistened with sweat. He held the object in his hands.

"All clear," he shouted. "It's an old carbide lamp."

Not a bomb. Freddy was thankful.

NOT A BOMB? Freddy was horrified.

People were walking home muttering. They weren't pleased at being saved but cross at being frightened. The air raid warden's face was pale and he was wiping his forehead with his handkerchief.

Mr Binstead was surrounded by the three policemen, getting a lecture about not wasting police time. Michael, having caught sight of Mr Binstead's face, was nowhere to be seen.

At last the policemen left Mr Binstead alone. He stood staring up and down the road as if looking for someone.

Freddy suddenly thought he'd better go home.

The South Road Army did not parade again for some time.

Freddy and the Spy

When the leaves turned brown and the mornings were misty and Daddy had nearly finished what he had to do in Africa, Freddy went away as well. For the first time, he stayed away from home without either of his parents.

Granny and Grandad Bassett asked him to go, so Mummy took him, first in a green train, then on an underground train, then on a long dark red train like the ones he had seen come through his own station two years before. Then she left him and came home on her own.

Granny and Grandad Bassett were different from Granny and Grandad Crake. Grandad Bassett was a big man with a loud voice and a large black moustache. Granny Bassett was tall and thin with short greying hair. Freddy liked her but wasn't too sure about him.

But the one living in the house that he really did like was his Uncle Jim, Daddy's brother. Uncle Jim laughed a lot, took him to a football match on his first Saturday there and slipped him threepenny-bits when no one was looking.

Granny and Grandad Bassett were very proud that Daddy was away at the war. Grandad Bassett only wasn't there, he was always telling Freddy, because he was too old.

"I did my bit in 1914," he kept on saying.

This surprised Freddy, because people were always on at him to do his every day, sitting on the lavatory seat. Cows, however, did theirs whenever they felt like

it, all over the field. Cats covered theirs up. Sometimes, as he watched Grandad Bassett smoking his pipe and reading his newspaper by the fire, he wondered whatever his insides must feel like if he hadn't done his bit for nearly thirty years.

Uncle Jim wasn't at the war because he was in something which made Grandad Bassett very angry indeed. A "reserved occupation", it was called.

"He's in a reserved occupation," Grandad Bassett often said in tones that made it seem like a terrible disease.

Freddy tried to work out what it really was. There were a lot of clues around. "Occupation", he knew from the radio, was what the Germans were doing in France. "Reserves" were, so he had found out at school, what Red Indians live on. They had also – and this made it really puzzling – been playing football in the match Uncle Jim had taken him to.

Whenever he tried to imagine what Uncle Jim did every day, a lot of strange ideas came into his mind.

Meanwhile, Grandad Bassett seemed to get angrier and angrier about it.

"Reserved occupation my foot," he once shouted. "He's just a big pansy."

No, Grandad Bassett and Uncle Jim weren't getting on too well. When Jim was at work, Freddy often had to listen to Grandad Bassett's remarks.

"He's no good."

"He's just frit."

"He should be out there doing his bit like everyone else."

This surprised Freddy. The complaint must run in the family.

"He won't help us win the war."

The last statement, which Grandad Bassett thundered out to a silent and sad Granny Bassett, worried Freddy a lot. He decided he'd better talk to Uncle Jim about it. If Grandad Bassett were right, it could be serious.

He spoke that same evening, when they were on their own in the kitchen.

"Uncle Jim, why won't you help us win the war?" he said.

"Who says I won't?" said Jim.

"Grandad."

Jim looked cross.

"Oh. Well, anything he says is bound to be right, isn't it?" And with that he left the room.

From that moment, Freddy looked at Uncle Jim in a very different way. He had admitted that he wasn't going to help the war effort. He had confirmed that Grandad Bassett *was* a man whose word could be believed. Yes, this was serious.

Freddy thought of all the posters he saw on walls everywhere – about careless talk costing lives, of trusting nobody, however nice and innocent they seemed. It couldn't, surely, be that generous, laughing Uncle Jim was a Nazi spy ready to have them all killed in their beds? Freddy started to look for evidence.

Sometimes, after he had gone to bed, he heard voices raised downstairs. Once, he crept downstairs to listen.

Grandad Bassett and Uncle Jim were shouting at each other. Granny Bassett tried to get a word in edgeways.

Grandad Bassett: "I'm right ashamed of you."

Uncle Jim: "It's not my fault I've been kept back."

Granny Bassett, nearly crying: "Oh, be quiet, you two. I can't bear to listen to you."

Grandad Bassett: "Well, you'll have to. That he should let us down like this. He's no son of mine."

Uncle Jim: "You can think what you like. We'll see who laughs last. We'll see who wins in the end. Maybe you'll be very sorry one day."

Jim strode out. The front door slammed behind him and the whole house shook. Freddy scuttled upstairs, jumped into bed and considered what he had heard.

What about what Uncle Jim said? It was terrifying. Jim must mean the Germans were going to win after all and not the British. *How did he know?* And the very last words were a threat.

And then, look what Grandad Bassett said. Freddy was sure he hadn't misheard it.

If Jim wasn't his son, THEN WHO WAS HE?

Freddy jumped out of bed, dashed to the window and watched Jim's dark shape striding along towards the end of the blacked-out street. Where was he going? Who – and this was very worrying – was he going to meet? What would he bring back?

At breakfast next morning, Freddy hardly dared look at Jim for fear he would see a swastika armband on his sleeve. Grandad Bassett and Uncle Jim never looked at each other. Granny Bassett stayed in the kitchen, snuffling quietly.

When Jim had left the house, Grandad Bassett turned to Freddy.

"Never be like him," he said. "Always do your bit."

He's got it on the brain, thought Freddy.

Granny Bassett came in. Her eyes were red with crying.

I'm not surprised, thought Freddy. It must be awful to find out your son's a German spy.

"Why can't you two make it up?" she said to Grandad Bassett.

"How can we?" said Grandad Bassett. "He's gone too far this time."

All day, Freddy felt completely miserable. Uncle Jim had been so marvellous before; now he was a cold-blooded, treacherous enemy. He had taken Freddy to a football match before; now he was just as likely to put a bullet through his head or a knife through his heart.

And at six that evening, he'd be back, just like he always was.

But would he? What had Grandad Bassett said? "He's gone too far this time."

Now some really terrible thoughts flooded through Freddy's mind. Uncle Jim disappearing for ever; perhaps even now in a submarine or aeroplane headed for Berlin to tell Hitler all about our secrets.

Well, if that were so, at least he'd be out of the way. Freddy felt sudden relief.

It went away at once.

What if Jim *did* come back this evening? What if all that about going too far had just been an idea he'd planted in Grandad Bassett's mind? Because if Grandad Bassett thought he'd gone too far, then he wouldn't be expected back. There was no end to the cunning of spies. And if Jim wasn't Grandad Bassett's son after all, there was no telling what he might do.

And then it would be very clear who would laugh last. And Granny and Grandad Bassett wouldn't have long to feel sorry. Nor – he realized with sudden chill – would he.

But no. Jim wouldn't come back.

Six o'clock. A noise outside in the dusk. Freddy looked out of the window.

A dark figure stooped by the front door. It straightened up. Jim. A wooden box was at his feet,

obviously heavy from the way Jim had put it down.

Freddy caught his breath in sheer terror.

Jim turned his key in the lock. The door opened. He bent again to the box.

Freddy bolted downstairs, shouting at the top of his voice.

"He's come back. He's got a bomb. He's going to blow us up. Get the police."

Granny and Grandad Bassett were in the kitchen.

"What's up?" said Grandad Bassett.

"He's back. He *is* a spy. He's going to kill us all before he goes to Germany."

Granny and Grandad Bassett stared at Freddy wide-eyed.

The living-room door opened. They all turned. Jim stood there, the box at his feet.

"What are you talking about, Freddy?" said Granny Bassett.

Freddy had worked it all out.

"He's going to light the fuse. Then he's going to lock us all in and run for it. When we get blown up, he'll be in the next street."

Grandad Bassett stared at Jim.

"What have you got there?" he said.

"Peace offering," said Uncle Jim.

"No it's not," shouted Freddy desperately.

"It's a crate of beer," said Uncle Jim. "Eight lights, eight browns and eight stouts. Keep you going for a week, that will."

Grandad bent to look at it.

"Where'd you get this from?" he said suspiciously.

"Never you mind," said Uncle Jim.

Grandad had a closer look. He found a label on the side and peered at it for a long time. Then he straightened up.

"You'll get yourself shot for this," he said.

"There you are," shouted Freddy. "I'm right. Grandad thinks so too."

Freddy could never understand why Grandad Bassett and Uncle Jim burst out laughing, why they embraced each other and said sorry, why the biggest smile of joy he'd ever seen split Granny Bassett's face and why the last week of his stay was one of the best times he'd ever had.

But then, he didn't try to understand. He just enjoyed it.

Freddy and the War Games

A few months after Freddy came back from Grandad and Granny Bassett's, some sad news came from Grandad Crake. Granny Crake was very ill. Mummy was upset. She went to see her, leaving Freddy at home. Of course, Freddy didn't have to stay in the house all on his own. Mummy made arrangements for him to be looked after. When he heard what they were, Freddy wasn't too pleased.

He was to stay with Michael.

Since the episode with the bomb that wasn't, Freddy hadn't seen very much of Michael. Michael now went to the Senior School. From afar, Freddy noticed Michael wasn't the big boy among the little kids any more. He was now the smallest of the big ones. Freddy nearly felt sorry for him. But not quite. He couldn't help remembering when Michael had been the Great Leader.

Before she caught the train, Mummy took Freddy along to Michael's house. Inside, all the rooms were in the same place, so Freddy soon found his way around. But the furniture was different and the colours were different and where everything was put was wrong. At first he was cross and wanted to say "You can't put that there" when he saw the wireless on a table and not on a shelf and the sideboard under the window and not opposite the fireplace.

Then he looked out of the window. It was still South Road that he saw. But he was on the wrong side, his own house stared back emptily and he felt he had made a longer journey than Mummy had.

He was to sleep in a little low bed made up in Michael's room. Michael slept in a big bed opposite. From where Freddy lay, its counterpane looked like the side of a big, pink ship.

On the first evening, he had his supper with Michael and his parents; then they all listened to the wireless; then it was time for the boys to go to bed. Upstairs, Freddy lay silent, thinking about Mummy and feeling sad. Michael interrupted his thoughts.

"We're going to play British and Germans and you've got to be the Germans."

A feeling of great weariness descended on Freddy.

I might have known it, he thought. There's no point, but I may as well ask.

"Will we take turns at being German?"

"No. It's my house so I'm British all the time."

That means, Freddy thought sadly, that he's going to win all the time.

The game started. First of all, Freddy was flying a German bomber.

"You're a Heinkel crossing the Channel," said Michael. "I'm leading a squadron of Hurricanes."

"All right," said Freddy sulkily.

"Well, do something," said Michael.

"What?" said Freddy.

"Fly the Heinkel," said Michael.

Freddy sat up, put his hands in front of him as
if holding a steering wheel and made half-hearted
aeroplane noises.

"Scramble scramble," shouted Michael. "Red
Leader to C for Charlie. Bandits one-zero. Tally-ho.
Over and out."

Freddy stopped the aeroplane noises.

"What?" he said.

"Shut up and keep flying," said Michael.

Freddy started droning again.

Michael now made frenzied Hurricane and
machine-gun noises.

"Eeeeyyyyaaaooooowwww. Er-er-er-er-er-er."

Freddy kept on droning.

"Got you," shouted Michael. "I've shot you down. You're dead."

"No," said Freddy. "You missed. I've baled out. I'm floating down with my parachute on."

"No, you're not," said Michael confidently. "You've gone down in flames. You're just hitting the sea now. Now you're flying the second bomber."

"But …" began Freddy.

"Er-er-er-er-er," yelled Michael. "Got you again. Down you go."

"How can I …?"

"Er-er-er-er-er. That's the third. I'll shoot down the lot of you."

"That's not fair," said Freddy.

"Of course it is," said Michael. "Do you *want* London to get bombed?"

"No," said Freddy. "But …"

"Well then," said Michael. "Shut up while I shoot you down."

When twenty-seven Heinkels were at the bottom of the sea, Michael said, "I'm tired. I'm going to sleep now."

Even his breathing had a note of triumph in it.

Freddy lay looking at the ceiling, feeling cross and homesick by turns.

Next night, Michael said, "All right, Freddy. Tonight we'll swap round."

"You mean I can be British?"

"No, you can fly the fighters. I'm the crew of a Lancaster over Berlin."

"But …" began Freddy.

"What's the matter? I'm giving you a chance, aren't I? You can be flying Messerschmitts. You see all the Lancasters and you come in to shoot them down. It's easy for the fighters because they're small and fast and the bombers are big and slow. You've got to get them before they start dropping their bombs."

"What do I do?" said Freddy.

"You fly over the Lancasters waiting for a chance to jump them," said Michael. He was sitting up in bed and gripping the controls of the Lancaster. "Enemy coast ahead," he said. "Watch out for flak. Target to starboard. Making my approach now."

Freddy listened to him.

"Come on," said Michael irritably. "Attack us."

Freddy started Messerschmitt noises like Michael's Hurricane noises. His machine guns were even louder.

"Eeeeeaaaayyyyooooowwww. Er-er-er-er-er."

"Bandits to port," shouted Michael. "Get him, rear gunner. Chaka-chaka-chaka-chaka-chaka. *Got him.*"

"I've shot you down," said Freddy.

"No, you haven't. My tail-end Charlie got a perfect bead on you. You're going down in flames. Now."

"That's not fair," said Freddy.

"Try again," said Michael. "You can be a whole squadron of Jerries."

"Eeeeeaaaayyyyooooowwww," said Freddy. "Er-er-er-er-er."

"Missed," said Michael. "Chaka-chaka-chaka-chaka-chaka. Got you."

"I'll never shoot you down at this rate," said Freddy.

"Of course you won't," said Michael. "Don't you *want* Berlin to get bombed?"

"Yes," said Freddy.

"Well, then," said Michael.

By the time Michael's rear-gunner had shot down nineteen Messerschmitts, Freddy was fed up.

"I'm going to sleep," he said.

"Coward," said Michael. "Typical Jerry."

"Why can't I fly a Spitfire?" said Freddy.

Next night, Freddy tried to go to sleep straight away. Michael wouldn't let him.

"All right, you *can* fly a Spitfire tonight," he said.

"Are you going to be German, then?"

"No. I've thought of a much better idea than that."

I might have known it, thought Freddy.

"We're both in this squadron of Spitfires. I'm the leader. And everyone thinks you're British. But you're not. You're German and you've tricked your way into the RAF and you keep shooting our planes down from behind while you pretend to be one of us."

"But don't the Jerries try to shoot me down?"

"No, because they know all about you so they leave you alone. But I find you out."

"How?" said Freddy.

"You can't speak English properly."

"That's silly," said Freddy. "Anyone would spot that."

"No, you're *quite* good. But there's just one thing gives you away. And I'm the one who notices it. You can't say water."

"Why not?"

"Germans can't."

"What do they say, then?"

"*Vorter.*"

"Why?"

"They can't say 'w'."

Michael made "w" sound like a rather snappy dog.

"Why not?"

"Well, they can't, that's all."

"Have they got a different sort of throat?"

"I don't know."

"But if they can't say 'water', they can't say 'window' or 'Wednesday' or 'wobble' or—"

"All right," said Michael. "Don't make a meal of it."

"And if he can't say double-u at all, anyone can tell he's German."

"This one can. Except 'water'."

"Why 'water'?"

"Because if he could, I wouldn't know he was German."

There was something wrong with this reasoning and Freddy tried hard to work it out. For Michael, though, the argument was over. He was making Spitfire noises again.

"Red leader to C for Charlie," he shouted. "Are you receiving me? Over."

"What?" said Freddy.

"C for Charlie. That's you. The Jerry," said Michael. "You've got to start talking so I can rumble you."

Freddy thought.

"You're supposed to be flying a Spitfire," said Michael.

Freddy made a Spitfire noise and thought.

At last he spoke.

"I'm thirsty," he said. "Can I go downstairs and get a glass of vorter?"

"That's no good," Michael spluttered in disgust. "You're supposed to be flying an aeroplane."

Freddy tried again.

"Ooh, there's the sea," he said. "Look at all the lovely blue vorter."

"That's no good either," said Michael. "You aren't in the Spitfire to look at the view."

"Well, what can I say, then?"

"Perhaps your radiator's leaking."

"Have Spitfires got radiators?"

"They must have."

"All right," said Freddy. Spitfire noise for a few seconds, then – "My radiator's leaking. The cockpit's full of vorter."

"Ah!" shouted Michael in triumph. "You're a Jerry. I knew it all along. I was only waiting for you to give yourself away. This is the end for you, my friend."

But before he could go into his machine gun routine, Freddy interrupted.

"Just a minute," he said. "If I knew I couldn't say 'water' properly, I'd make sure I never said 'vorter' to you."

"Yes, you would," said Michael. "Because you're stupid."

"I can't be stupid if I got in the RAF and fooled you all these years."

"But I found you out," said Michael.

"It took you long enough," said Freddy.

"I've had my suspicions for a long time," said Michael.

"You mean I've been shooting your planes down all this while and you've only had suspicions?" said Freddy.

"Oh, shut up," said Michael. "Go to sleep."

Freddy made some machine gun noises himself.

"Er-er-er-er-er-er-er-er. That's finished you off. Down you go. Now you're in the vorter. I'm off home to Germany."

That night, he slept like a log.

Michael was quiet and tight-lipped at breakfast. He

went off to school without a word. Freddy spent the day feeling faintly pleased.

That night when they went to bed, Michael was still silent. But just when Freddy thought sleep would be allowed to come straightaway, he spoke.

"Tonight," he said, "we're playing Invasions. You're the Jerries still and I'm the British and the Americans and the Russians and everybody else. And I've got millions of soldiers and guns and ships and tanks and planes and I'm going to sort you out once and for all. You haven't got a hope."

"That's not fair," said Freddy.

"Yes it is," said Michael. "Everything's fair in war. Besides, you started it."

"No, I didn't," said Freddy. "You did. You thought of all the games."

"You started the war. Everyone knows that."

"Well, it doesn't matter," said Freddy. "I'll still win. All my soldiers have got secret death-ray guns and they can kill all yours just by pointing them."

"That's *really* stupid," said Michael. "Death-ray guns haven't been invented."

"Well, wait a minute while I invent them," said Freddy.

"Don't talk rubbish," said Michael. "We're only playing about what *could* happen. The invasion's starting now. We're coming at you through France and the Russians are coming through Poland. You won't last long."

"But I *have* got a secret weapon," said Freddy. "I've got a lot of inventors and they've just invented it."

"I don't believe you," said Michael. "We're coming in NOW!"

"You come one step further and I press the button," shouted Freddy.

"What button?"

"This one."

Freddy jabbed his forefinger at the iris of a Michaelmas daisy printed on the wallpaper.

"And then what will happen?"

"All your forces will be blown up and so will you."

"You can't have a weapon that will do all that," said Michael. "If you could, it wouldn't just blow us up. It would blow up the whole world."

"I don't care," cried Freddy recklessly. "It will blow *you* up. That's all I want."

"But you'd be blown up as well."

"Doesn't matter," said Freddy.

Michael sat up in bed. His face was white with anger.

"You're spoiling the game," he shouted.

"I'm stopping you winning," replied Freddy.

Michael jumped out of bed. He crossed the room.

"We'll see who's going to win," he said threateningly.

He reached out and seized Freddy's right wrist.

"Ow!" shouted Freddy.

Michael reached out for the other one. Freddy pulled it away from him and reached out with his forefinger towards the Michaelmas daisy and let it stay poised above it. "I'm going to press the button," he shouted.

"I won't let you," yelled Michael. He seized Freddy's left wrist an inch away from the wall.

Freddy struggled. His finger was nearer and nearer …

"Nearly there," he gasped.

"You wouldn't dare," grunted Michael. His face was red with effort.

With a superhuman push, Freddy managed the last inch. His finger landed square on the iris and stayed there for three seconds before Michael could pull it away.

"That's it," Freddy shouted in triumph. "I've pressed the button. We're all blown up. You, me, the

lot. There's nothing left. The game's over. You've lost."

Michael let got of Freddy's wrists. He stalked off back to his own bed, threw himself on it and pulled the bedclothes up sharply.

"These games are silly," he said.

"I only made them up to take your mind off things while your mum's away. I might have known it would be no use doing something sensible for a little kid."

"I stopped you winning, didn't I?" said Freddy.

He felt really pleased with himself. Once again, he slept contentedly till the sun through the window woke him up.

Next day, Mummy came back.

"Hullo, Mum," said Freddy.

She looked at him in surprise for a moment. Then:

"Granny's dead," she said. "You must come with me to the funeral."

Freddy and the Meccano Set

On Christmas Eve, Freddy woke up with a funny feeling in his tummy.

Am I ill? I couldn't bear to be, he thought.

No, he wasn't ill. It was a looking-forward-with-fear-of-disappointment feeling. Next day, he would have a Meccano set. He *knew* he would.

"But you know there's a war on, Freddy," said Mum. "They don't make them any more. All the steel goes into tanks."

This was true. They'd even taken away the school railings for tanks. They couldn't even spare the last six inches of railing, which would have yielded enough steel to make a huge Meccano set. And Mum's saucepans were now flying around as part of a Spitfire.

The war was a terrible thing.

Especially now that Dad, having gone through North Africa ("like a dose of salts," Grandad Bassett said proudly) was with the army somewhere in Italy. *He* would have found a Meccano set.

Freddy got up early to put up the paper chains. Long evenings he'd spent painting bits of paper, cutting them in strips and pasting them together in gaudy, unequal links. He'd had to be patient to finish them – but it was worth it if it earned him a Meccano set.

Grandad Crake, who had come to live with them after Granny Crake died that April, helped him.

"Got to pass the time till I go to see what sort of a chicken that twister of a butcher's got for us," he said.

As he stood on a chair sticking the end of the chain up with a drawing pin, Freddy dreamed of his Meccano set. There would be long green strips and girders, red plates, pulley wheels, gear wheels and wheels which had real rubber tyres to fit on. If his set was *really* large there would be cylinders and a boiler in grey. And the things he could make! He'd seen a catalogue. On the cover was a picture of two boys just finishing off a car *which looked as big as Mr Binstead's Morris 8 laid up for the duration of the war.* It was only an out of scale drawing, though – he couldn't really expect to make the family a car they could go for trips in, even if it was powered by the No. 2 Clockwork motor.

But there were photographs as well. Two especially. The Baltic Tank Locomotive and the Hammerhead Crane. The Baltic Tank was a huge railway engine with massive driving wheels and connecting rods made entirely from all those little parts screwed together. And nearly big enough to let you sit on the rear bunker and be pulled along. While the Hammerhead Crane was even better; the sort that newsreels at the pictures showed brooding over the River Clyde making ships for the navy.

The Supermodels, the catalogue called them.

Marvellous, thought Freddy. By the time Christmas is over, I will have made a Supermodel.

Grandad Crake wasn't much help with the paper chains. He just grumbled all the time. When they had finished, and Grandad Crake had said for the last time, "It's not as good as when I were a lad," it was midday.

"I'm off to the butcher's," Grandad Crake called to his daughter. "I'll bring the bird back for plucking. I might call in at the pub on the way."

Before he went, Grandad Crake ate some bread and cheese. Mum mashed two potatoes and boiled some cabbage for herself and Freddy.

"Must eat up all the scraps before Christmas," she

said. She looked round the room. "Freddy," she said. "You've made it look really nice."

"I'll make you all sorts of things with my Meccano set," he said.

"Don't bank on it, love," she answered. "There's a war on. Father Christmas can't manage everything."

"I *know* he'll bring me one," said Freddy, looking hard at his mother. He was quite prepared to go along with her about Father Christmas if it would help his cause.

"I wish we had a tree," said Mum. "Your father always used to get us a lovely tree. We've not had one since he went in the army."

"They make aeroplanes with them," said Freddy.

No part of his surroundings, it seemed, was safe.

Mr Binstead had a fir tree, overhanging the garage which contained the laid-up Morris 8. And the Binsteads were away for Christmas. What if he took his father's saw out of the shed, crept round the back and sawed a branch off? That, with the paper chains, should ensure a Meccano set.

He imagined the scene: Mum's gratitude, Grandad's awe at his resource.

No. Mum would be furious with him. And the branch, stuck upright in a pot, would look silly. And there'd be nothing to decorate it with. And Mr Binstead would notice when he got back and would come round complaining. And the Meccano set, *if* it lay hidden somewhere in the house, would most likely stay there.

Difficult.

When he had eaten, he went out in the frosty air to visit Stella, Tony and Barry, Kathleen and Janet, Mavis and Enid, Philip, Reg and Tom. He didn't go to Michael's. Together, they swopped forecasts of what the next day's hauls might bring. He came home in the freezing dusk sure he would do the best of them all.

Grandad Crake entered the house at the same time. Freddy noticed the beer smell so knew he would be happy. Grandad Crake gripped a limp feathered form by the neck like a trophy won at enormous odds. They entered the lighted kitchen together; Grandad Crake flung the bird on the table and said to Mum, "I'll draw and you pluck."

Freddy didn't like watching this bit; he departed to the living room and put the radio on. The Christmas edition of *Much Binding in the Marsh* was interrupted by a howl of rage from the kitchen. It was followed by the foulest smell Freddy had ever known.

In the kitchen, Mum and Grandad Crake looked aghast at the bird, its insides all over an oilcloth sheet on the table. The smell, it was clear, came from them.

"The crook. I'll kill him," shrieked Grandad Crake. "He's done us out of our Christmas dinner."

"Perhaps he didn't know, Dad," said Mum.

" 'Course he knew. He never killed this bird. It died of old age. Or a belly-ache."

"What are we going to do?" said Mum.

Grandad Crake quivered with rage.

"I said that butcher was a twister. Don't you worry – I know things about him he doesn't know I know. I'll get a proper bird off him."

Grandad Crake bundled the remains, oilcloth and all, into a sack and trudged off into the night. Mum kept the kitchen door open. The cold came in as the smell went out.

"Oh dear," she said. "That wouldn't have happened if your father had been here."

Grandad Crake came in two hours later. He was smiling. He carried another limp feathered form.

"This one's all right," he said.

"How did you do it?" said Mum.

Grandad Crake tapped the side of his nose with his forefinger and winked.

"I *know* things," he said. "This bird's all right."

And it was. Relief replaced the memory of the smell.

Night drew on. Freddy parcelled up and addressed the tiny gifts and home-made cards he had prepared for Mum and Grandad Crake and put them on the mantelpiece. Then he went to bed and tried to sleep.

Would he get a Meccano set? Had he done enough to ensure one? If he instead of Grandad Crake had forced a proper chicken out of the villainous butcher, would that have made the difference?

But if they weren't making Meccano sets because of the war, then surely there was no hope.

He went to sleep with the sheer misery of this thought. In his dreams, the Baltic Tank Locomotive and the Hammerhead Crane disappeared like mirages.

When he woke, it was pitch dark. He sat up and felt a chill round his shoulders. He lay down again and reached out with his foot. It touched something hard. A full pillowcase. He kicked at it. The sound was that of hollow wood with a slight metallic jangle.

He held his breath. *Could* it be?

He switched the light on. Mum's voice called from the next room.

"Freddy, I don't suppose for one moment that Father Christmas has brought you a Meccano set, but if he has don't get the nuts and bolts all over the bed."

Freddy couldn't speak for excitement. He pulled the pillowcase towards him. There were small packages at the top which he put by for later. At the bottom was a large, black wooden box with a label. MECCANO. *The toy that engineering made famous.* Underneath was a picture of that same Hammerhead Crane. For a full minute, Freddy stared at it in rapture; then, slowly, he took the lid off.

They were all there, in little compartments. Strips, girders, plates, wheels, tyres. There were even cylinders and a boiler in sinister grey. The red and green paint was, he saw, chipped. Well, what matter if the set was second-hand? It was *here* and it was *his*.

He opened the instruction manual. The models weren't quite as big as the Baltic Tank Locomotive. He thought he'd try a motor-bus first.

Following the instructions turned out to be hard. The pictures looked flat; he couldn't see how one thing fitted to another. The writing was in a strange clipped language which didn't seem to make sense. The list of parts required was full of numbers he didn't understand. The parts themselves were hard to identify. The nuts and bolts were fiddly and – what would his mother say? – got all over the bed.

He discarded the bus. He tried the Mechanical Man, who looked easy. But it had just a pulley wheel for a head and Freddy couldn't make the model move at all, though the instructions promised that it would. Freddy decided that the mechanical man was stupid.

Now he discarded the instruction manual. I'll make a model up myself, he thought.

Not so easy. He decided to put tyres on the wheels and make a car. Whatever it was that he finally bolted together looked like nothing on earth. None of the parts seemed to fit properly. Then the nuts came undone and the whole thing fell to pieces.

By now, he was nearly crying. He turned over on his side in frustration and lay right on a gear wheel which had strayed on the sheet. His shout of pain brought Mum running.

After that, he turned to the other presents. He felt very unhappy. He couldn't bring himself to look at the Meccano set and the wrecks of his efforts. He found a new book and read until he got up.

The day passed quickly. The chicken was lovely. So was the pudding. They all drank a toast to the King – Grandad Crake in brown ale, Mum in elderberry wine and Freddy in lemonade.

"Let's remember my old lady," said Grandad Crake.

They did.

Then they remembered Dad in Italy and drank to him.

Mum cried.

She's crying for Dad, thought Freddy, and cried too.

The King's broadcast ended. The tears were dried.

"Where's the Meccano set?" said Mum. It was the first time she had mentioned it.

"Upstairs," said Freddy.

"Bring it down," said Grandad Crake. "Let's see what you can make with it."

Unwillingly, Freddy did so. He dropped bits on the stairs as he came down. Already, the neatness of parts laid out in their compartments was but a memory.

"Make something," said Grandad Crake.

He opened the instruction manual and pointed to a contraption with one wheel and two strips sticking out at the back – *wheelbarrow*.

More tears from Freddy.

"I can't do it," he said. "It's too hard and fiddly."

"When I were a lad …" Grandad Crake began, but then stopped. Mum was crying again.

Freddy looked at her. And then realization dawned like a white light. Yes, he'd done the paper chains. Grandad had got the chicken. And those things weren't bad at all to have done. BUT MUM, SOMEHOW IN TIME OF WAR, HAD WANGLED HIM A MECCANO SET. What could she have gone through to get it? And all because it was the one thing on which he had set his heart.

And now, making things with it was too hard for him. He'd let her down. She'd done it all for nothing.

The tears started again.

"I can't stand this," said Grandad Crake. "When do the pubs open?"

"You'll learn, Freddy," said Mum. "You'll learn in the end."

It was time for tea and Christmas cake. Then the radio – *ITMA* and *Waterlogged Spa*. So Christmas Day ended. The Meccano set was taken back upstairs and Freddy slept.

He dreamed again about the Baltic Tank Locomotive and the Hammerhead Crane. They gleamed red and green. The intricacies of their making mocked him. When he woke on Boxing Day, their images stayed with him.

The black Meccano box was the first thing he saw. He jumped out of bed, opened the box and looked at the jumble of parts. Then he spoke to the Baltic Tank Locomotive and the Hammerhead Crane as if they were in the room with him.

"I'll make you," he said. "I'll make you one day. You see if I don't."

Freddy and
the Prisoners of War

Christmas dropped away behind them. The New Year sped on and suddenly Spring arrived. With it came a letter which made Mum cry, Grandad Crake happy, Grandad and Granny Bassett write letters Freddy couldn't understand at all but which made Mum happy again.

Dad had been taken prisoner by the Germans in Italy.

Granny and Grandad Bassett came to stay for a while when they heard the news. Though Uncle Jim wasn't with them, the house nearly burst at the seams.

"He's safe now," said Granny Bassett. "He's not going to get killed."

"He can have a good rest," said Grandad Crake. "He deserves it. The Jerries will look after him. They know what'd happen if they don't."

"Don't you be too sure," said Grandad Bassett. "I can tell you a few tales about what went on in the last war."

"What about the Geneva Convention, then?" said Grandad Crake.

"You don't know *nothing*," said Grandad Bassett.

The two grandads had never got on, ever since Mum's wedding day.

It wasn't so much that they were all happy that Dad wasn't fighting any more or that they were sad that he wasn't doing his bit any more. ("That's daft," said Grandad Bassett. "He's *done* his bit.") It was just that, before, they all had some idea of what he was going through. They saw newspaper photographs, newsreel films at the pictures; they listened to the wireless. They picked out places in the atlas. They gleaned what they could from his few censored letters. They always had some idea of what things were like for him and could at least be with him in their thoughts.

But now their imaginations failed. Freddy dreamed at night of a starved man, all skin and bone, dragging a steel ball chained to his foot. A giant with a whip stood over him.

"He will be safe now, won't he?" said Mum.

It was a good question, but there was no one to answer it.

Stella was a clever girl. Even in the days of the South Road Army Freddy had been slightly in awe of her. And she had been the first in the class to be able to read. She was still the first to do anything.

Now she was first in the class for something else.

Her father had joined the Navy. The ship he was on had been torpedoed by a U-boat and sunk. He was dead.

For a week she was away from school. When she came back, she was quiet and wouldn't let anyone cheer her up. But nobody knew how to anyway.

New people were coming. In the evenings the streets were full of different soldiers. Their uniforms were lighter in colour than Dad's or Mr Binstead's Home Guard tunic and made of smoother material. Their stripes were smaller and upside down; sergeants had little pyramids sewn on their arms, not big letter Vs. Their boots were soft and brown and they wore funny squashy hats. They were American.

They were very friendly. They spoke to people without being asked to. Once, one of them said to Freddy, as he came out of a shop with Stella, "You got a pa, son?"

"Yes," said Freddy.

"Is he in the war?"

"Yes. He's a prisoner in Germany."

The American soldier ruffled his hair and said, "Don't you worry, son. We're going to get him out."

Stella said nothing. The soldier looked at her and seemed to know why.

"We're going to make it up to *everybody*," he said.

For days now the roads were choked with army lorries, armoured cars and tanks, all going south towards the sea. The roar of tank tracks and motors and of aeroplanes overhead kept them awake at night. It seemed a very big effort just to get Dad out of prison camp.

Freddy watched the tanks; one after the other, some with Americans on board, some with British. Each tank had a big white star painted on it. Then, one day

in early summer, they stopped coming through and there weren't nearly so many Americans in the town. But with such a huge rescue party being formed, Freddy felt close to Dad.

There were other new arrivals. But they didn't come into the town. Freddy and Stella were walking along the road which passed Farmer Crellin's outlying fields when they saw them. A group of six men, their backs bowed, repairing fences. They wore shabby grey tunics with a yellow circle stitched on the back of each one. A soldier with a rifle stood guarding them. He motioned Stella and Freddy away.

One of the men looked up and stared straight at Freddy.

Freddy's stomach turned over and his legs felt like water.

The man was exactly like his father.

"Da …" he started to call. But he cut the word off at once.

The man showed no sign of recognition. His face was lined and bitter. Voices murmured. Freddy knew they were speaking in German.

"I'm frightened," said Stella. "Let's go home."

Mum was weeding in the back garden when he returned. Grandads Crake and Bassett were there as well, arguing. Granny Bassett sat in a deck-chair, trying not to listen. Mr Binstead was digging his garden next door. Freddy told them what he'd seen, without mentioning Dad's German double.

"German prisoners of war," said Mum. "A few are allowed to work on farms. You must keep away from them."

Mr Binstead heard.

"A waste of good food," he shouted over the fence.

"We can do without that lot. If I had my way, they'd all be shot. Serve 'em right after what they've done to us."

Mum ran indoors, crying.

"Oh, sorry," said Mr Binstead. "I forgot."

"He's a right twerp," said Grandad Crake.

"He ought to be shot himself," said Grandad Bassett.

At least they agreed for once.

Freddy dreamed most nights now of his father in a grey tunic working by the side of a road and lines of tanks with white stars on them coming to take him away. And at the back of his dreams was the face of Dad's German double – thin, lined, stubbly-chinned, but with the bitterness in the eyes replaced by yearning at the thought of the many miles between him and his home.

Freddy and Stella were often together now. They were the two children in the class so far most touched by the war. They spoke little to each other – and certainly never about their fathers. But just being together was a consolation.

One day in late May they were walking together in the fields behind South Road. Freddy knew deep down that he was looking for the German prisoners so he could see his father's double once more. But he was never to see them again.

They stopped at the bomb crater, now completely overgrown.

"Do you remember that night?" said Freddy.

"I wasn't even scared," said Stella. "I thought it was all a big game."

They crossed a stile and were in Farmer Crellin's fields.

Haymaking was going on. Stella and Freddy scrambled through a hedge and found themselves face to face with a man with a tanned face and shiny black hair. He wore an open-necked shirt, brown breeches and boots. He swung a long-handled scythe easily and cut the long grass off neatly at the roots.

The two looked at him in horror. The same thought came to both of them – that they were caught trespassing and Farmer Crellin would have them both up in court.

Stella spoke quickly. "We lost our way," she said. "Sorry, mister."

"*Scuse?*" said the man. "You not do wrong. You stay and talk."

They stared at him.

"Where are you from?" said Freddy.

"Me? From Italia. Marco from Milano. What you call Eyetie. Wop."

"But …" began Freddy. He stopped and looked at this laughing man so completely at home in an English hayfield.

"Yes," said the man. "We fight you once. Now, all stopped. Italia leave war. This country and us, we like *that* together now."

He laid one forefinger over the other so it made a cross.

Freddy looked at the fit, happy man. It couldn't be …

"You're a prisoner of war," he burst out.

"Si," said Marco. "P.O.W. Out of the war for ever. Once, big, dangerous man. Now I work for farmer because you and Italy big friends now and everyone trust me."

"How long have you been here?" asked Stella.

"In England, three years. On farm, two months. I like it. I taken prisoner by British in Africa."

Once again, Freddy's stomach turned and his knees buckled.

"Where in Africa?"

"Tobruk."

Silence again. Almost the first word Freddy learnt to read.

"Did you see my father?"

Another silence. Then Marco said quietly, his eyes downcast and sad, "Yes, I see him OK. But I not recognize him."

Another silence, while they realized Marco had been reminded of something he would rather forget.

"Where your father now?" Marco said at last.

"A prisoner. Taken by the Germans in Italy."

Somehow, Freddy found this very difficult to say to Marco.

"Is all right," said Marco. "He safe now. Being prisoner is OK. I have good time."

Freddy didn't answer. He remembered the other prisoners, sullen, with circles on their backs, Dad's double among them. He wished he could see them again and say to them, "Being prisoner is OK. You safe now."

"Where you live?" said Marco. "What your names?"

Freddy told him.

"I bring you something good," said Marco. "From Italia. Something you like."

"You shouldn't have told him that," said Stella as they walked home. "The grown-ups won't like it."

Freddy couldn't understand this.

"We're friends," he said. "We trust him."

"They won't like it," repeated Stella.

From then on they seemed to see Marco every time they went out. He lived in a room in one of Farmer Crellin's tied cottages, empty while the war was on. He told them about Italy, about his family, about how one day he would go home.

Then, one day: "I say I make something good for you. Soon now. You very good to me. You cheer me up. So I make it for you and your people."

"What does he mean?" said Stella.

They soon found out. One Sunday there was a knock at the front door.

"Go and see who that is, Freddy," said Mum.

Freddy opened the door. Marco stood there, with a big china bowl covered with a cloth.

"I make for you. Like I said. Spaghetti Milanese. Very good. You eat it."

"Who is it, Freddy?" said Mum. She came to the door and saw.

"You take it. You eat it. Enjoy," said Marco.

Mum looked embarrassed.

"It's very nice of you, Mr – er … But I don't think …"

"You take. For you. Because Freddy good to me. Stop me being lonely."

Grandad Crake came to the door.

"You Eyeties," he said. "Get back where you belong."

"I want to," said Marco.

Freddy stood silent, creased with shame.

"Well, I don't know," said Mum doubtfully.

Marco looked down at the ground.

"You don't want it?" he said. "I do it all for nothing. You will not take it because you say I am prisoner still."

Freddy spoke at last.

"Let's take it, Mum," he said. "Marco's nice. And it smells lovely."

Mum looked at Marco and smiled suddenly.

"Thank you very much, Mr – er … It's very nice of you. We'll enjoy it. Won't you come in and share it with us?"

"I no come in. It is not right. I go back to farm. You enjoy. *Buon appetito.*"

And he was gone, disappearing up the road with long strides.

Grandad Crake looked disgruntled.

"I won't eat that foreign muck," he said.

Mum took the cloth off.

"But where did he get all the stuff to do it with?" she said. "He didn't find these things on the ration."

"Farmers and Eyeties," said Grandad Crake. "They're all the same. All twisters. Like that butcher." The Christmas chicken still rankled with him. "All on the fiddle."

"It's going cold," said Mum. "I'll heat it up."

"Flush it down the lav," said Grandad Crake.

"I'll do no such thing," said Mum.

"Well, I'm not touching it," said Grandad Crake. "You should have sent him packing."

"I didn't want to hurt his feelings."

"*His* feelings?" said Grandad Crake. "What about mine? I'm off down the pub. Don't bother to keep any of that slop for me."

So Mum and Freddy ate the lot. It was lovely – strange, spicy and rich – and as they ate the spaghetti was splattered all over the place.

"That was the best Sunday dinner ever," said Freddy. "I wonder if he took one to Stella's house as well?"

"It's better than we would have had otherwise," said Mum. "And I can save the meat ration for another day."

Grandad Crake came home. He looked regretful, especially as he sniffed the fading smell of Marco's meal.

"Ah, well," he said. "I suppose you shouldn't look a gift horse in the mouth."

Yes, Marco did take a bowl to Stella's house. Her mother cried her eyes out when he'd gone. But they enjoyed it.

Next evening, Stella and Freddy took the bowls and cloths back. They reached Marco's cottage. But it was locked and empty and they never saw Marco again.

And then they found out where all the tanks and soldiers had gone to. D-Day came; the Allies landed in Normandy. The great expedition to bring Dad home was on.

Tony's father was killed on Juno Beach. Stella and Freddy had someone else to talk to.

Freddy and the End of It

Amazing things were happening in the world far away. Michael's final war-game was coming true. Allied troops were moving across France, Holland and Belgium from the west; Russian troops across Poland from the east. Freddy waited for the secret weapon.

It came. First of all, strange little aeroplanes with stubby wings and no pilots which flew across the sea, cut out suddenly in mid-air and then fell, to explode, because they were flying bombs. The "Doodlebugs" everybody called them and one fell on a field close to South Road.

It was quite frightening, but as a secret weapon, Freddy didn't rate it very high.

But the next one was different.

People came to the town from London with tales of sudden huge explosions which came without warning. These were made by bigger rockets which came from nowhere and nothing could stop them.

As a secret weapon, the V2, Freddy thought, was better. But

it didn't hold up the Allies and soon the V2s didn't come over any more either.

There was a feeling that before long everything would be over and the world would change. Freddy lived through these months in a state of suppressed excitement. He couldn't remember a time when there wasn't fighting, blackouts, ration books, dried eggs and dried milk, Utility symbols on the few things bought new and books printed on grainy paper with war economy labels.

But there was more to it than that. Freddy only knew the life he had led. Sometimes he wondered if there had ever really been a time called Peace. Perhaps, because he hadn't been there to see it for himself, it was just something the grown-ups said to cheer him up.

But it couldn't be. There was going to be something different. Grown-ups said so; Mum, Grandad Crake, even Mr Binstead.

"When this is over, we don't want to go back to those old times," Mr

Binstead once said over the garden fence to Grandad Crake.

Grandad Crake agreed.

"We want it better than it was after the last lot," he said.

This surprised Freddy – not only that Grandad Crake and Mr Binstead agreed about something (Grandad Crake had taken Dad's place completely as someone for Mr Binstead to be cross with) but also because surely peace was always better than war. If not, what was the point of it all?

And Mum said the same.

"When the war's over, Freddy, you'll have a better chance."

Better than what?

"Things are going to be a lot different," she added.

Different from what?

And then the war in Europe was over. There were pictures of generals in stiff peaked caps and shiny boots surrendering to generals in black berets and sloppy tunics.

Flags appeared on every house and wirelesses blared from every window. People danced in the streets and particularly all along South Road. The noise they made was drowned by another, which cut through the air and was unlike anything Freddy could ever remember hearing before. For a second, he thought his eardrums would burst.

"Church bells," said Mum. "The first for six years."

But as all this happened, Freddy saw other things,

which, like the V2s, came from nowhere to shock and disturb. Photographs in the paper and reports on the wireless which frightened him and made him feel sick. Bodies no more than skeletons piled up on top of each other; human wrecks, all skin and bone, with staring eyes, shuffling along in front of these piles. The end of the war was showing some terrible things. Like so much else, Freddy didn't understand them. But thoughts of the photographs kept him awake at night; sometimes as he lay in bed his whole body shook with an anger he could not explain.

Though there was still a war taking place on the other side of the world against Japan, everyone knew it would end soon. So something new and big and exciting was happening at home. An election.

Freddy only knew this was to get a new prime minister.

But why did we need one? Mr Churchill seemed healthy enough to Freddy.

"In peace time," said Mum, "we often have new prime ministers and governments. We choose a new one every few years."

Freddy couldn't quite see why. But all the posters and meetings and loudspeaker vans were very exciting – as was the fact that once again people were getting *really* cross with each other.

Mr Binstead and Grandad Crake especially. They argued over the fence; they argued as they walked together down to the pub; they argued with the greatest force of all late at night after closing time, on the pavement in front of their respective houses before they each went inside and slammed their front doors on each other.

"Mr Churchill's won the war for us," roared Mr Binstead. "He deserves a proper go in peace time. You're just an ungrateful, unpatriotic, treacherous old git."

"And there's a few million like me," shouted Grandad Crake. "When have his lot ever done a thing for the likes of me? Or you either, if it comes to that? We want to give the other lot a chance. Up the workers, that's what I say."

This time, the two slammed doors sounded as loud as the bomb which made the crater five years before. Next morning, Grandad Crake sat at breakfast looking very happy.

"I've not had a real good argument since 1939," he said.

That evening, Freddy listened to *Much Binding in the Marsh,* his second favourite programme (the first was *ITMA*). At the end of it, in their closing song, Richard Murdoch and Kenneth Horne put a verse in about the election.

They thought that if you put an x,
The thing would be a draw.

Freddy laughed. Though he didn't quite see the point.

One day, every grown-up put an "X" on a piece of paper and the day after, all the winners and losers were announced on the wireless. Grandad Crake was overjoyed at the results. Mum said to Freddy, "Now you're bound to get your chance in life." Mr Binstead looked over the garden fence and said sourly, "Misery ahead; you mark my words."

"I think your father will be quite pleased," said Mum.

Only two days after the election, Mum said, "Your father's coming home next week."

Freddy was sitting on the floor surrounded by bits of Meccano. He really had got the hang of it by now. He was making a big six-wheeled lorry. He had worked out a way to steer it properly with a steering-wheel in the cab. The chassis was nearly built and the two front wheels and four back wheels with their thick rubber tyres looked really good. If only, he was thinking just as Mum spoke, they were making motors to put in them – clockwork or electric, he didn't care which – and, whenever they did, that he could afford one.

Mum was holding a letter. Her eyes were sparkling.

Freddy looked at his model.

"I'll finish it for him," he said.

The week passed; the lorry was built; the election was forgotten. A small group of people waited on the station platform: Mum, Freddy, Grandad Crake, Grandad Bassett, Granny Bassett, Uncle Jim. They stood without talking, peering away down the track towards where it became misty with distance and where bridges looked like toys with little matchstick people walking across them. The minutes went like hours; the station clock seemed to have stopped.

Then, with a clank, a signal arm shot upwards. They all jumped. Time slowed even further.

Freddy strained his ears.

"OOOORRRRP!" he heard faintly.

Then, far away, a little plume of smoke; a black dot ever enlarging; at last, clearly, the big green train puffing, clanking, snorting and spitting towards them.

Slam of doors, chatter of people, hiss and drift of steam – and then Dad was with them, wearing a

baggy blue suit and carrying a little suitcase. His sandy hair was thinner, his face was lined and his eyes were deep. He was hardly smiling, but deep contentment radiated from him. Freddy remembered with painful clearness the German prisoner he had seen last year and found himself wondering if he was at home yet and as happy.

When they were all able to think again, Dad looked at Freddy.

"I don't believe it," he said. Then – "There's so much to do and say."

But somehow, on that platform in the weak morning sun, no one could say another word.

They walked home together joyful and close. Still no one spoke – not until they were inside the house.

As they entered, Freddy looked across the road and saw Stella watching through an upstairs window.

And then they were inside

"I like the lorry," said Dad.

Summer drew on and Freddy became used to life being something like what it always should have been. They all went away for a few days for a holiday by the sea. The barbed wire was gone; Freddy could go in the sea at last. He sat in it as the waves scurried up the sand past him and sucked their way back again and he looked forward to years of holidays and life with no more cares.

The sun shone on his back; seagulls cried; Mum and Dad sat on the beach together watching him and he thought: I want this moment to last for ever.

It didn't. They came home. And the very next morning the wireless and papers were full of different news. A bomb had been dropped on a city in Japan so powerful that everything in it had been destroyed in one go. Next day, another was dropped and another city was destroyed. One bomb each. One aeroplane. No one on our side hurt.

Freddy never forgot the first thing he thought.

"That means the war's really over," he said.

"What a way to end it," said Dad. "We'll never sleep safe again."

"Why not?" said Freddy.

"Because if they can drop it on them," said Mum, "they can drop it on us."

"We'll drop it back," said Freddy.

"Much good that will do us," said Mum.

Freddy remembered once again the war games with Michael. Now they were coming true completely.

"Anyway," he said. "This war's over."

"Thank God," said Dad.

And this time it really was. Another day of celebration – and Freddy, with Stella and Barry and Tony and Mavis and Enid and Michael and all the rest, were in the thick of it. For the first time in their lives they saw fireworks. The whole thing seemed worth it just for that.

So Freddy went to bed that night very happy. But into his dreams came visions of whole cities burning and living skeletons shuffling along in front of piles of dead ones and when he woke up and his dream was forgotten he was troubled but could not say why.

Millions of people lived through the end of the war and never forgot it. Freddy lived through it with them and, now he was nine, would not forget it either. But another life was starting and he was ready for it.

Some other exciting books
from CATNIP PUBLISHING

Robert Westall

A TIME OF FIRE

The sky split open. A sky of brilliant yellow light; a world of noise that filled his ears like sand at the seaside, so that afterwards there was only total silence.

It takes just a few seconds for the German bomber to drop its deadly explosives and disappear into the clouds. But those few seconds change Sonny's life for ever. In the months that follow Sonny finds himself pursuing his own dramatic and intensely personal confrontation with the Germans.

'*Deeply moving...Strong, uncompromising writing*'   Telegraph

Robert Westall

THE MAKING OF ME

A writer's childhood
Edited by Lindy McKinnel

'Fascinating scenes from Westall's childhood, and insights into the development of a fine writer. A lovely book.'
David Almond

'A collection of Robert Westall's writings, allowing us a glimpse into his thoughts – on growing up on Tyneside during World War 2, on life and death and most of all, offering an insight into the imagination of a great writer'
Valerie Bierman

Sid Fleischman

PIRATES GALORE

Hidden treasure, heroic last stands and hairbreadth escapes!

Plucked from the sea after a storm, twelve-year old cabin boy Shipwreck just wants to get home. But his rescuer is the most infamous pirate in the Pacific – and his adventure is only just beginning!

A rollicking tale of secrets, betrayal, revenge and lost loves by Newbery Medal winner Sid Fleischman